The Boy Who Longed for a Lift

by NORMA FARBER

pictures by

BRIAN SELZNICK

A LAURA GERINGER BOOK
AN IMPRINT OF HARPERCOLLINS PUBLISHERS

The Boy Who Longed for a Lift
Text copyright © 1997 by Thomas Farber
Illustrations copyright © 1997 by Brian Selznick
Printed in the U.S.A. All rights reserved.
Library of Congress Cataloging-in-Publication Data
Farber, Norma.
The boy who longed for a lift / by Norma Farber ; pictures by Brian Selznick.
p.   cm.
Summary: A boy gets tired of walking and accepts lifts
from many sources, but the one from
his father as he arrives home is the best.
ISBN 0-06-027108-6. – ISBN 0-06-027109-4 (lib. bdg.)
[1. Hitchhiking–Fiction.   2. Stories in rhyme.]
I. Selznick, Brian, ill.   II. Title.
PZ8.3.F224Bo 1997   95-35936
[E]–dc20   CIP
                                        AC

1 2 3 4 5 6 7 8 9 10
❖
First Edition

The text was hand lettered
by Brian Selznick,
based on the typeface
Nicolas Cochin Roman.

For my sister Holly Spector,
her husband Ed,
and all of Holly's students

~ B.S.

The boy went walking one fine day,
walking, walking, a long, long way.
He grew quite tired, so he cried,
"Who'll offer me a ride?
Who'll carry me far and wide?"

A brook came flowing, soft and swift,
and gave the boy a lift.
The boy said, "Whether fast or slow,
this is the only way to go!"

But even for a boy so bold,
the brook was really far too cold.
The shivering boy turned blue and cried,
"Who'll offer me a ride?
Who'll carry me far and wide?"

A boat came sailing, light and swift,
and gave the boy a lift.
The boy said, "Whether fast or slow,
this is the only way to go!"

But what a slender, tipsy ship!
It tossed and turned and did a flip!
The boy got scared, and so he cried,
"Who'll offer me a ride?
Who'll carry me far and wide?"

A trout came slipping, sleek and swift,
and gave the boy a lift.

The boy said, "Whether fast or slow,
this is the only way to go!"

No sooner said than trout was gone,

with boy just barely hanging on.

"Oh, you're slippery! Help!" he cried.

"Who'll offer me a ride?

Who'll carry me far and wide?"

A snail came creeping, far from swift,
and gave the boy a lift.
The boy said, "Whether fast or slow,
this is the only way to go!"

He murmured, "Snail's no racing horse,
but safe to travel on, of course."
He soon grew bored, he yawned and sighed,
"Who'll offer me a ride?
Who'll carry me far and wide?"

There came a horseman, galloping swift,
and gave the boy a lift.
The boy said, "Whether fast or slow,
this is the only way to go!"

There's such a thing as too much speed.
Before he had a chance to plead,
a tree got fastened in his hair,
and held the boy up in the air.
He dangled high and said, "Oh no,
this is no proper way to go!"

He gazed at clouds meandering past,
and said, "I'm going nowhere fast."
He rubbed his head and loudly cried,
"Who'll offer me a ride?
Who'll carry me far and wide?"

A white gull swooped down, bright and swift,
and gave the boy a lift.
The boy said, "Whether fast or slow,
this is the only way to go!"

But hardly had the flight begun,

when boy and gull flew near the sun.

"Ow! I'm getting burned!" he cried.

"Who'll offer me a ride?

Who'll carry me far and wide?"

The rain rained down in silver pails,
and let him ride on silvery rails.
The boy said, "Whether fast or slow,
this is the only way to ~ OHHH!"

The rain rained swiftly down and yet
the boy complained of being wet.
"Just drop me please! That's it! You tried!
I do not want so damp a ride."

The boy went walking, that fine day,
walking, walking, a long, long way.
He grew quite tired, but walked some more

till finally he was home.

His father ran out, strong and swift,

and gave the boy a lift.